Lily's Dressing-Up Dreams

The Flowered Apron

Lily's Dressing-Up Dreams

The Flowered Apron

JENNY OLDFIELD

Hodder
Children's
Books

A division of Hachette Children's Books

"This is so not fair!" Pearl complained.

First Amber had been whooshed off into Cinderella world. Now Lily had had her turn at being Snow White.

"How come I haven't been magicked?"

"Listen," Lily told her. "If you want to know the truth, Snow-White world is seriously scary. There's this dark forest outside the palace gates. And the Queen is

Wicked with a big fat capital 'W'!"

Lily remembered with a shudder how Queenie had wanted to kill her when the magic mirror said that Snow White was the fairest in the land.

"I don't care. I still want a go!" Pearl declared. "Where's the mirror? Is it in the pocket of that cloak you're wearing?"

"No. It's hanging on the Queen's wall." Lily had whooshed back from her fairy-tale world in a dazzle of bright light, still wrapped up in a dark red velvet cloak with a warm fur lining.

Now Amber wanted to hear every detail of her magical adventure. "What was the palace like?"

Lily took off the heavy cloak and dropped it in Amber's dressing-up box.

"The palace was dark and cold."

"Did you meet anyone nice?"

"The Nurse was on my side. But Prince Lovelace was a geek. The King seemed OK, but I didn't see much of him."

"What about the dwarves?"

Oh yeah, Snow White and the Seven Dwarves, Lily realised. "I didn't actually meet them," she told Amber, while Pearl tried on the Snow White cloak.

"Twirl," Amber told her. "If you're to be magicked, see if it whooshes you off."

Pearl held her arms out wide and started to turn on the spot. Soon she grew dizzy. But the room hadn't changed and there was no bright light.

"Nothing!" she sighed, taking off the cloak and flinging it back in the box.

"Let's dress up anyway!" Lily suggested.

"How do I look?" Amber demanded as she tried on her granddad's hippie waistcoat. It was made from purple velvet with silver embroidery.

"Rubbish!" Pearl cried.

Lily was too busy dipping into the box to notice. "What's this? It looks like a witch's broom."

"From last year's Halloween costume," Amber explained.

"Sweep-sweep!" Lily said, taking the broom and happily brushing the floor.

"Watch out!" Amber warned as a shimmering white light suddenly surrounded Lily.

"Sweep-sweep!" Lily tidied the cellar.

"Uh-oh, it's happening!" Pearl cried, as

the dazzling light blinded her and Amber.

"Dah-da-di-dah, da-da!" Lily sang. She liked cleaning – always had.

"Lily's vanished!" Amber gasped.

"It's *so* not fair!" Pearl's voice wailed as Lily whooshed off into Snow-White world.

"Tarrum-tum-tum!" The dwarves sang their marching song as they trekked through the dark forest.

When Lily woke up from a deep sleep, she was lying on one of the seven beds in the cottage in the forest. "Ohhhh, I'm so tired!" she yawned.

"Watch where you swing that lamp, Hans!" a voice called. "You just knocked it against a branch and brought down a

heap of snow on my head!"

"Stop moaning, Tom," Jack told him from up ahead. "We're almost home. Can't you see the light ahead?"

"I'm ready for my supper," Roly sighed as he trudged through the deep snow. He pictured meat pie with a crumbly golden crust and a mountain of mashed potatoes swimming in gravy.

"It's sure been a long day," Pete agreed. "Digging for gold is never easy."

"Like moles under the ground," Will added. Trudge, trudge in single file, every step taking them nearer to the cottage.

". . . So tired!" Lily yawned, sitting up.

"Tarrum-tum-tum!" Seven voices sang in the dark as Jack, Tom, Roly, Pete, Will, Hans and Walt made their way home.

2

"There's nothing I like better than a nice, big meat and potato pie!" Roly declared as the dwarves' cottage came into view. "Out of the oven and served piping hot!"

Jack smiled as he led the way into the clearing. "You're always thinking about food, brother!"

"With carrots covered in rich gravy," Roly sighed happily.

"Just a second – I spy someone else who might be fond of carrots!" Pete interrupted. He'd spotted Lily's grey mare half-hidden behind the woodshed. She'd tied her there before she'd crept into the cottage to investigate then fallen asleep on one of the seven beds.

"Where did she come from?" Pete said.

The mare lifted her head and neighed.

"She wasn't there when we left home this morning." Walt sounded puzzled. "It looks like we have a visitor."

Will hurried towards the cottage and opened the door. "Who's there?" he called.

Suddenly Lily wasn't tired. She jumped from the bed to peer out of the tiny window.

13

One, two, three, four, five, six . . . silently Lily counted the dwarves in the small clearing. "Seven!" she said out loud as she saw Hans fumble with the mare's rope.

"Steady, girl!" Hans tried to soothe the frightened horse. But she pulled at her rope and broke free.

"Watch out, Hans!" Tom warned.

Too late. The mare set off at a gallop across the clearing. She bolted into the forest.

"Oops!"

"Hans is a clumsy so-and-so!" Tom tutted.

"There goes my horse!" Lily gasped. "Now how will I get away from here?"

"Who's there?" Will called again. "Come out and show yourself!"

"What I do is hide!" Lily told herself. She dived under the nearest bed and held her breath.

"That's strange," Will muttered when

15

no one answered his call.

The seven dwarves filed through the
door and seven pairs of eyes scanned the

empty kitchen. They put down their seven
pickaxes and kicked off seven pairs of
snow-covered boots.

Help! Lily thought from under the bed.

She heard seven sets of footsteps drawing nearer.

Please magic me out of here! Now Lily could see lots of feet, all wearing darned socks, and sturdy legs dressed in woollen leggings. The feet disturbed a thick layer of dust on the old floorboards. The dust drifted up her nose – "Aaah . . ."

Walt sat on his bed. The springs in the mattress creaked. The whole bed sank towards the floor.

". . . Chooo!" Lily sneezed.

Walt sprang up as if he'd been shot. Jack dived under the bed and dragged Lily out.

"It's a girl!" Will said, looking at dusty Lily in her red velvet cloak and Spanish leather boots. "Well I never!"

3

"Tell us truly how you came to be here,"
Jack said to Lily as the dwarves sat her
down to supper. "When we've heard your
story, we will decide how to help you."

"That smells good!" Will said as Roly
opened the oven and produced an
enormous pie. He cut into the pastry and
served supper. "And now, my little
princess, we will eat and while we do

18

you must tell us your tale."

Munch-munch. The seven dwarves ate heartily.

"I'm not really a princess," Lily began.

"But you live in the palace," Pete said with his mouth full. "You ride a fine horse and your name is Snow White."

"Don't interrupt," Jack warned Pete. "Be patient. Listen."

"I didn't *choose* to live there," Lily pointed out. "It just kind of happened." Then she hesitated. How did you explain to seven strangers that you'd been magicked out of your own world into the world of Snow White? *Better not try*, she thought. "Anyway, for whatever reason I'm stuck there and Queen Serena doesn't like me."

"Ah, Her Most Royal Highness!" Will said quietly.

Jack, Tom, Roly, Pete, Hans and Walt all shook their heads and tutted.

"Yes, HMRH," Lily nodded. "I mean, she really doesn't like me. In fact, she hates me!"

"Because she is jealous," Pete added quickly.

Lily stared at him. "How did you know that?"

"It is well known," Jack explained. "The new queen has a mirror on her wall. Each day she goes to the mirror and asks who is the fairest lady in all the land. She is only satisfied if the mirror replies with her name, saying, 'Thou, Queen, art fairest in the land!' If not, and another name is spoken, Queen Serena will set out to destroy her rival."

Eagerly, Lily nodded. "That's right. That's exactly what happened with me. That's why I ran away into the forest."

"It is because you are such a fair child," gallant Will explained. "With skin as white as snow and hair as black and glossy as the raven's wing."

Lily blushed.

"Tut-tut," sensible Tom interrupted with a grin. "Beware of Will's silver tongue!"

"It is true," Walt told her with a slow, warm smile. "You are the prettiest girl in the land!"

"Even though I hid under your bed and scared you?" Lily asked him. "Are you sure you're not angry with me?"

The other dwarves smiled. "Walt is never angry," they said. "He is the most amiable among us."

"And Pete is the cleverest," Will explained to Lily. "Jack is the boldest by far. He leads wherever we go. Tom is the one you can always rely on – steady as the rock under our feet. And you cannot argue with good-natured Roly . . ."

". . . Unless you keep me from my supper!" Roly grinned as he scooped up the last of his gravy.

"True enough," Will nodded. "And as for Hans, he is not one of Nature's most graceful creatures. In fact, there is hardly a tree trunk in the forest he has not bumped into or a root he has not tripped over!"

"True," Hans confessed. "And I have the bruises to prove it."

"And what about you, Will?" Lily wanted to know. She loved learning about the gang of brothers with the merry, twinkling eyes and smiley mouths.

A pity about their clothes, she thought to herself, recalling the big holes in their socks and their saggy, badly-patched leggings.

For once, Will was slow to reply.

"Ah, Will!" Jack supplied the answer.

"Our brother Will can charm the birds from the trees."

"Hush!" Will said, embarrassed. "Continue with your story, Snow White. What exactly happened after Queen Serena learned that you were fairer far?

"My Nurse, Gretchen, overheard Queen Serena talking to one of her huntsmen. They were plotting to bring me into the forest and kill me." Lily wanted to hurry through the scariest part of her story. She was upset by the memory of Sir Manfred, the huntsman's thin, harsh face and the Queen's sinister plot.

Kind Hans gasped. "How could anyone be so cruel?"

"Well, I wasn't going to hang around and wait for it to happen," Lily explained.

"Gretchen told me about a friend beyond the forest – the Queen of Ice Mountain – so I set off to find her."

Tom nodded eagerly. "I have heard that she is a kind lady. But she lives far away and the journey is full of danger."

Pete agreed. "The forest is so thick that in places you cannot pass. In others, there are hidden shafts leading to the gold mines deep underground. My dear Snow White – if you fell down such a hole, you would disappear, never to be seen again."

Lily gulped.

There was silence, before Walt spoke up, his face glowing in the lamplight. "I have it!" he declared.

All eyes turned to him.

"Speak, brother!" Jack urged.

Walt's eyes sparkled. He spoke slowly, as if surprised by his own cleverness. "Snow White, you must stay here with us!"

Lily looked around, waiting for the dwarves' reaction.

Six heads nodded in agreement. "That is a wonderful plan, Walt! . . . Of course! . . . Brother, you are right!"

Walt's kind face was wreathed in smiles.

"Good. That's settled then," Jack said, standing up and starting to clear away the dishes. "My dear, you shall have a room and a bed all of your own. And if the Queen's wicked huntsman should come searching for you, we will hide you and keep you safe, never fear!"

26

4

And so Lily went to bed that night in the tiniest room at the back of the cottage. She slept well between fresh sheets smelling of lavender, under a warm patchwork quilt, while outside the snow fell and silence ruled over the dark forest. The next day, Lily woke with the rising sun.

She tiptoed to her door and called down the corridor. "Hello – is anybody there?"

There was no reply. And there were no pairs of boots lined up by the front door, no pickaxes leaning against the wall.

A note on the table read: "Good morning, Snow White. Please make yourself at home. See you later. Love from, Jack, Tom, Roly, Pete, Will, Hans and Walt xxxxxx . . . X"

Wow, they go to work early! she thought. *"Make myself at home"* – hmm!

There were dirty dishes in the kitchen sink, so Lily washed and dried them until they sparkled. Then she found a broom in a cupboard and began to brush the dusty floors.

Sweep-sweep. *Dah-di-da-di-dah!*

Clouds of dust rose up and flew out of the door. Small birds chirped in the trees.

A butterfly fluttered across the clearing.

"Aaaah-choo!" Lily sneezed as she picked up a feather duster and whisked it along shelves.

Now what? she wondered, at midday, when the cottage was spick and span. She went into the dwarves' bedroom and found a pile of socks, each one with holes in the toes and heels. Then she discovered a needle and thread. Soon she was busy singing and mending. *Dah-di-da-di-dah!*

The sun shone in through the cottage windows, bees buzzed, bluebirds sang.

By mid-afternoon all of the socks were darned.

"What next?" Lily hummed to herself as she wandered restlessly around the cottage. Then she caught sight of herself in a mirror and glanced down at her grubby embroidered gown. "Huh, that's what comes of clearing up in your best dress!"

The stains bothered Miss Neat and Tidy Lily. "What I need is a nice big apron," she decided, hunting in drawers for a piece of old fabric which she could tie around her waist. *Da-di-dah* . . . She pulled out a large square of flowered cotton

30

which matched the faded curtains at the cottage windows. The fabric had a pattern of big yellow and white daisies against a bright blue background. "Here's just what I need!"

And scissors and sewing pins, plus the needle she'd used to darn the socks. Carefully Lily gathered everything she would want.

Da-di-da-di-dah! Snip-snip went the scissors, in and out through the cotton cloth went the sharp needle.

"Almost finished. Now for the long ties."

Lily was so busy making her apron that she didn't notice the sun setting between the tall trees, or the silence in the forest as the birds took to their nests for the night.

"Tarrum-ta-tum," the dwarves sang as

they approached the end of their long trek home.

Dah-di-di-diddy-dah! The flowered apron was finished. Lily tied it around her waist and looked in the mirror to admire it. She twirled.

"What was that?" She'd heard a faint noise – perhaps a man's voice. Was it the dwarves returning home?

No, there was the sound of a horse's hooves too, and the baying of dogs.

Lily ran to the cottage door and peered out. Dusk had fallen without her noticing. The forest was full of moving shadows.

Then she saw the figure of a man on horseback, followed by three lean grey hunting dogs. The man had a thin face and a pointed beard. He shouted to the dogs to follow a scent.

"Sir Manfred!" Lily gasped. Terror seized her and threw her mind into a spin.

The Queen's man had tracked her down. Now he meant to kill her.

Lily cowered beside the door, hearing

the rider brush against branches as he and the dogs drew nearer.

"Snapper, Vixen, Storm – come to heel!" Sir Manfred yelled at the dogs as he noticed the clearing. He dragged at his horse's reins to point her towards the cottage.

Bolt the door! Lily told herself. Her fingers trembled as Manfred approached.

"Come out of there and show yourself, whoever you are!" the wicked knight ordered. "I see smoke curling from the chimney, so I know that someone is at home!"

Lily's heart thudded so loudly that she was sure Manfred must hear it.

"If you don't come out, I will break down the door!" he yelled, dismounting from his horse and rattling at the latch.

"Tarrum-ta-tum!" the dwarves sang as they slogged through the forest, their lanterns glowing yellow, their feet sinking deep in the snow.

The three dogs barked and snarled. Sir Manfred thumped with his fist at the cottage door.

"Hold!" Jack cried when he came into the clearing and saw the stranger. "Sir, have patience. There is no need to break down our door!"

His brothers lined up alongside him, pickaxes at the ready.

"Ah!" Manfred turned to face them. "Tell me – what do you know of a young girl from the palace who, according to the scent followed by my hounds, came

this way late last night."

Inside the cottage, Lily held her breath.

Tom stepped forward. "We know nothing, and we saw nothing," he insisted stoutly.

But Pete stepped in front of his loyal brother. "Indeed, there was a girl," he told the knight. "I saw her when I collected wood from the shed. She rode by on a grey mare, but she did not stop."

"B-b-brother!" Walt protested quietly. But before he could attract Sir Manfred's attention, Jack drew him firmly into the background.

"Describe her to me," Manfred told Pete.

"Very young, very pretty," Pete said. "With skin as white as snow and hair as black as the raven's wing."

"Snow White!" Sir Manfred hissed, drawing his sword from his belt. "On pain of death, you must tell me – which way did she go?"

"By the trail we have just come," Pete explained. "I'm sorry to say that we have trampled over her tracks and so your dogs may not be able to pick up her trail. And the forest is full of danger after dark. I feared she would come to harm."

"But you did not try to stop her?" Manfred asked, his cruel eyes narrow with suspicion. "You let her ride on?"

Pete nodded. "I would hardly risk my own life going after a stranger," he pointed out coolly.

"Very well." Manfred decided Pete was telling the truth. Lowering his sword, he remounted his horse. "Tell me – precisely what harm might befall Snow White in the forest?"

"There are wolves," Tom suggested. "They roam in packs, we hear them howling at the moon."

Still listening from inside the cottage, Lily shuddered.

"Entrances to mine shafts," was Roly's

idea. "Some are hidden by thick undergrowth. A girl may fall down one and starve to death."

"Fast-running streams covered over by ice," Will added. "And then there is the snow on the mountains, falling thick and fast. In the morning it loosens in the warmth of the sun and slides towards the forest. The girl is most likely buried under an avalanche, even as we speak."

"Enough!" Sir Manfred put up his hand, pleased by the many dangers Snow White had faced. "Surely she will succumb to one of them!"

"Oh, she'll be gone by now," Pete assured him. "You and your dogs are wasting your time, believe me."

"Maybe," Manfred snapped back. He

whistled Vixen, Storm and Snapper to him. "From what you say, it seems that I face possible death if I pursue Snow White further."

"*Certain* death!" Jack insisted. "Sir, I would advise you to return to the palace now, before it is too late."

Sir Manfred nodded. "You are right – I will leave off my search and return."

"We wish you well, sir," Jack concluded through gritted teeth, brushing past Sir Manfred and his dogs.

Vixen snapped at Jack's heels. Storm and Snapper growled viciously as his six brothers followed.

"And good riddance!" Roly added under his breath as Sir Manfred spurred his horse forward on his homeward journey.

5

"Today we will stay at home to watch over you," Tom told Lily over breakfast.

Lily had slept badly, afraid that Sir Manfred would return. Her face was pale and tired.

"We will take care of you," Jack assured her. "No more cleaning and mending, for you are a princess, used to having servants and handmaids. Today you must let us do the work in the cottage."

"But I *like* dusting and sweeping!" Lily protested. She put on her flowered apron and picked up the feather duster. "This may sound weird, but I can't just sit around doing nothing!"

"You may help me make dough for the bread," Roly offered.

"Or you may study how I mend the boots on an iron last," Will told her. "But first I must buy more nails in town."

"Aha!" Pete said with a wink in Will's direction. "Nails indeed! Ha!"

Ignoring his brother, Will put on his leather waistcoat and set out alone.

"Snow White, come to the door!" Walt called. "That's Hans hammering away."

"What's he doing?" Lily asked.

42

"He says it's a secret."

Tap-tap-tap went the hammer in the woodshed. And all through the morning there was no sign of Hans.

"Soup for lunch!" Roly announced. "Come and get it!"

"Yum!" Lily was having a great day after the terror of Manfred's visit the night before. There were flowers in a vase on the window ledge, brought in by Walt from a low meadow, and the kitchen was full of the scent of Roly's freshly-baked bread.

"I'll go and tell Hans," Lily said.

Quickly she slipped outside, breathing in the fresh air and knocking lightly on the shed door before she went in.

Lily found Hans hunched over a bench where a tiny object sparkled between his broad hands. "Da-rom-pom-pom!" He sang a song and turned a small lathe.

Lily crept forward to see better.

"Pom-pom, pom-pom!"

A fine gold chain coiled on the rough wooden bench, and beside it lay a polished gold locket set with tiny diamonds that sparkled like stars in the sky.

"Oh!" she gasped.

Hans jumped and almost fell off his stool. He turned and blushed.

"It's beautiful!" Lily sighed, looking over Hans's shoulder. The diamonds formed two tiny letters inside the golden heart – "S" and "W" – "Snow White!"

Hans moved to one side. "I meant it as a surprise," he said quietly.

"It's lovely!" Lily said, wondering how

Hans's clumsy fingers had fashioned something so delicate.

"It's a present," Hans explained. He smiled shyly and offered her the necklace.

Lily hung it round her neck.

"From us all," he added. "To tell you that you are welcome, Snow White, and may stay with us for ever."

"For ever?" Lily echoed, her fingers brushing the locket as it nestled against her neck.

Will came back from town just as the soup bowls were being cleared from the table.

"Now, brother – did you fetch the 'nails' to mend the boots?" Pete asked.

The others laughed then nudged and winked.

"Here!" Will produced the nails from his pocket. There was a frown on his face as he plonked the paper bag on the table.

"Are you sulking?" Tom asked. "Come, Will – now that you have a girlfriend you must get used to being teased."

"Her name is Melina," Jack explained to Lily. "She works at the palace."

"Ah!" Now Lily understood Will's blushes and frowns. "No wonder he was so eager to go to town on his day off!"

Jack nodded and smiled.

Will shrugged. "It is no laughing matter," he grumbled. He took a steady breath and announced, "I have heard some news today."

"From the palace?" Pete asked, growing suddenly serious.

"Melina told me that the palace is in mourning," Will went on, looking steadily at each of his brothers. "King Jakob has ordered everyone to wear black for a year and a day. There must be no music, no feasts, nor any hunting."

"But why?" Lily demanded.

Will looked up. "Because Queen Serena has announced that you, Snow White, are dead!"

"Ah!" A satisfied sigh ran around the table. It seemed that Pete's clever plan had worked.

"Lost in the forest and now dead,

beyond the shadow of a doubt," Will insisted. "As we know, the Queen sent her huntsman, Sir Manfred, to search for you and he returned late last night with the sorrowful news."

"But how could Sir Manfred *prove* I'm dead?" Lily asked. At that moment she felt very much alive – her heart pounded, the hairs at the nape of her neck stood on end.

"Her Most Royal Highness has shown the King a piece of torn velvet," Will explained. "Sir Manfred took the fragment to the Queen and swore it was from the cloak you wore when you vanished. It is the proof he needed."

"But it's a lie!" Lily cried. "He made it up!" She pinched her arm. "Ouch! I'm definitely not dead – see!"

Jack held up his hands and asked for calm. "Let's think," he said. "This news from the palace is what we hoped for."

But all Lily could think of was poor King Jakob dressed in black and praying in the chapel, and Nurse Gretchen weeping in Snow White's empty chamber.

"Let the Queen believe it," Jack insisted. "Her Most Royal Highness will be *content* to think that you are dead, Snow White. She will believe that she has got rid of her rival as she intended."

Lily nodded. "And so she won't send Sir Manfred out to look for me any more?"

"That's right," Pete agreed. "But still you must take care, my dear."

"You must never open the door to strangers," Tom insisted.

"Or trust any who journey through the forest," Roly added.

"And then you will be quite safe," Hans assured Lily. "You may sleep well at night."

So Lily drew breath and was calm, sitting by the fireside as the afternoon passed and turned to evening. She sewed napkins for the seven brothers out of scraps of the same flowered cloth she'd used for her apron, humming quietly as the dwarves mended broken windowpanes, strengthened locks and made their cottage safe from intruders.

6

"Remember, you must keep the cottage door firmly bolted," Jack told Lily as the brothers set off early next morning.

"No need to remind me," she replied. The very thought of Sir Manfred sent a shudder down her spine. So she bolted the door, put on her flowered apron and busied herself around the cottage.

But once the dwarves had departed, the

day ahead seemed empty and long.

"There's only so much sweeping and dusting a girl can do!" Lily sighed as the sun rose and the bluebirds returned.

"Surely it would be OK for me to open a few windows to let in the fresh air," she said as the deer came back to graze.

A bee flew into the cottage through an open window. It buzzed angrily from room to room.

"Uh-oh, I'd better open the door to let it out," Lily decided.

The sunny air was so warm when she opened the door that she took a stool from the kitchen and sat outside happily mending a rip in one of Hans's shirts.

"It's His Most Royal Highness King Jakob that I feel sorry for," a woman's

53

voice said as footsteps approached.

Swiftly Lily jumped up from her stool and ran inside. She bolted the door then ran to a window to peer out.

Soon two women gathering firewood appeared. They stooped to pick up sticks to add to their bundles.

"Grief fills the King's days now that Snow White is dead," the first woman continued. "They say he neither eats nor sleeps – only hangs his head in sorrow."

The second woman paused in the clearing to ease her back. "It breaks a man's heart to lose his daughter," she sighed. "Kings and princes, rich though they are beyond our wildest dreams, suffer the same as the rest of us!"

"Except for the Queen," the first woman argued. "Her Most Royal Highness shows no sign of sorrow, but goes about the palace dressed in jewels and satin. Her step is light after her stepdaughter's death, though I hear her harsh temper is not improved."

"Hush!" the older woman warned, seeing that the windows to the cottage stood open. "Someone may hear you."

Inside the cottage, Lily stepped back from the window, pressing against the wall until the women had passed.

Trust Queenie to get away with it! she thought. She pictured Serena dishing out orders, swanning around in her sapphires and emeralds, happy that she was once again fairest in the land.

Lily knew that was a close shave. The two women might easily have discovered her. Perhaps it was best to lock up the cottage until the dwarves came home.

Flick-flick! Lily dusted every corner as the afternoon crept by. "I like cleaning, but not this much!" she sighed.

She sewed buttons on to Hans's shirts and patched the knees of his baggy leggings. "I like mending, but in the end even I get bored!"

Then Lily saw that the flowers in the jar on the window ledge were beginning to wilt. *Wouldn't it be nice for the brothers to come home to fresh flowers?* she thought.

She knew there were big white daisies growing in a meadow not far away, beside purple harebells and pink campion.

Surely I can nip outside for five minutes . . .

Lily passed through the forest then crouched among the flowers, carefully picking the daisies.

Horses came galloping through the trees. She dropped her posy and ducked down behind the tall flowers.

"The King will be displeased!" a voice

shouted. "Sir Manfred, come back – King Jakob has ordered that we may not hunt for a year and a day!"

Prince Lovelace! Lily recognised the high, nerdy voice. *And worse still – Sir Manfred!*

Ping! An arrow shot across the meadow and thudded into a tree trunk.

The knight himself soon rode into view. "Who will tell the King that we go against his wishes?" he sneered over his shoulder. "After all, Prince Lovelace, a man must have some sport!"

"Stop!" the Prince pleaded, catching up with Manfred on his sweating horse. The two men had ridden hard through the forest and both mounts gasped for breath. "Let us rest here a while!"

Sir Manfred took in his surroundings.

"See the cottage up the mountain?" he said to Prince Lovelace. "That is where I gathered news of Snow White. A slow-witted dwarf told me that the stupid girl had ridden on into a blizzard in the dead of night, and so I learned she was dead."

Not so much of the "stupid"! Lily thought as she crouched low.

"Yes, very stupid!" Prince Pester-Face agreed. "And disobedient."

Huh? Isn't this the Prince who pestered me wherever I went? Lily recalled. *Wasn't he all over me like a rash?*

And now she took another peek at Pester-Face, she remembered he was the worst geek, with his goggly eyes and big, bent nose, not to mention his silly voice!

"Well, good riddance to Snow White!"

Manfred declared, taking another arrow from his quiver.

"Yes, good riddance!" Prince Lovelace echoed weakly. "Snow White is nothing to me now. Today I have a new love in my life – Princess Ursula of Ice River!"

"Princess Ursula – your new love?" Manfred sneered. "Why, man, you change your affections as often as your socks!"

"Do not mock!" Pester-Face protested

angrily, just as another rider approached.

Quickly Manfred turned his horse to face the hurrying newcomer. Then he bowed low. "Greetings, Your Most Royal Highness!"

In her hiding place among the flowers, Lily held her breath.

"Stop bowing and scraping, you idiot!" Queen Serena yelled. Her fur cloak flew out behind her, her gloved hands tugged at the reins of her fine black stallion. "You told me that the child was dead!"

"Indeed she is, Your Majesty." Sir Manfred's voice now trembled with fear.

"Did you not give me this proof?" From beneath her cloak, Queen Serena produced the scrap of velvet cloth.

The knight nodded. He began to see that

his own sneaky plan had come back to haunt him – how he had torn the velvet from one of his own tunics, rubbed it in the snow and produced it as false evidence of Snow White's death.

Still he tried to bluff his way through. "I truly believe it belonged to the cloak Snow White wore when she disappeared, Your Most Royal—"

"Be quiet, fool!" Serena shrieked. "The child is not dead – she is alive!"

And closer than you think! Lily thought, shrinking further into the flowers.

The Queen ranted on. "Alive! Manfred, you are a villain to bring me false news. I will have you thrown into the dungeon!"

"Have mercy, Your Majesty!" Flinging himself from his horse, Sir Manfred went down on to one knee.

"Alive, you fool! I have it on good authority, from the mirror on my wall."

"Your Most—" Manfred began again, but the Queen cut him off.

"The mirror tells me everything!" she screamed, her face ugly with anger. "I look into the glass and demand who is the fairest in the land? The mirror gives me its honest answer – it does not lie."

Amongst the flowers, Lily screwed up her face and closed her eyes. She felt as if there was a sword hanging over her and it was about to fall.

"With Snow White dead, the glass would reply, 'Thou, queen, art fairest in the land'." Queen Serena glared at Manfred, hardly noticing Prince Lovelace, whose skinny legs trembled inside his big riding boots. "But what did it tell me when I saw my reflection this very noon? Let me repeat what it said, word for word."

"Please, Your Majesty . . ." Sir Manfred still begged for mercy.

"'Thou, Queen, mayst fair and beauteous be!'" Serena recited, her voice turning brittle. She took a deep breath then delivered the final blow. "'But Snow White is lovelier far than thee!'"

7

It was as if the sun had gone behind a big dark cloud, as if the birds would never sing or the deer come again.

Lily returned to the cottage and waited for the dwarves to return home.

"I will leave no stone unturned!" the Queen had sworn as she rode out of the meadow with Lovelace and Manfred trailing behind. "I will search every blade of grass until Snow White is found!"

And now all Lily could do was wait and listen for Jack's footsteps leading the way home and the dwarves' cheery voices singing in the distance.

"Tarrum-tum!" The sound drifted through the evening air at last. Tramp-tramp-tramp went their feet.

Lily sprang to her feet and unbolted the front door. Relief flooded her as she saw the golden pools of light from seven lamps and seven smiles greeting her.

"Hurry!" she told the dwarves as they stood by the door taking off their boots. Then she told them of the Queen's angry visit, of how the magic mirror had given them away, and how Serena had sworn to leave no stone unturned.

"This is very bad news." Jack shook his head and hung up his jacket. "We must make a new plan."

"Don't worry, Snow White," Tom said kindly. "We will think of something."

"I'm off to the palace to see what I can discover," Will decided straight away.

"In the dark?" Roly asked. "Without having supper?"

"Yes, Roly," Will replied. "I intend to find Melina. She will tell me more."

"Take great care, brother," Hans warned. "Snow White has enemies out there. Do not fall into their hands."

"I'll be careful," Will promised, sounding cheerful as ever as he set off through the snow.

*

Jack, Tom, Roly, Pete, Hans, Walt and Lily waited. Stars appeared in the sky, twinkling like the diamonds in Lily's golden locket.

Wolves . . . Mine shafts hidden in the undergrowth . . . Harsh blizzards. Lily ran through the dangers of the forest at night.

No one thought of going to bed. Everyone sat up to wait for Will's return.

When the sun in the east tinged the dark sky pink Jack stood up. "We must go out and look for him," he decided.

"Let me come!" Lily begged. "I can help!"

Tom shook his head. "You must stay behind. You cannot come to the palace with us. It would be too dangerous."

Lily saw she must back down. The

68

dwarves were too worried about Will to have her tagging along. "When will you be back?" she asked Jack, who led the others into the clearing.

"When we have found our brother and can bring him back unharmed," he replied calmly. "Meanwhile, lock the door, my dear, and open it to no one!"

*

All alone, Lily saw the sun rise.

OK, so I didn't want to be a nuisance, she thought as she made the beds and raked out the ashes in the grate. *But no way am I sitting here doing nothing!*

"Lock the door!" Jack had told her in his firm voice.

I mean, in the real story, Snow White tries to do as she's told. But that was then – ages ago, in the olden days. This is now!

"Open it to no one!"

This is now. And these days, girls don't sit around. Take Amber. When she whooshed into Cinderella world, she kept on trying to escape from the creepy cellar. The Uglies were mean, but she didn't take it lying down – no way!

Lily opened a cupboard in the dwarves' bedroom and rooted around for a clean pair of leggings and some decent socks.

Well, me neither! she decided. *Sure, it's risky, but I can wear a disguise.*

She put on the yellow leggings and red socks then found a red shirt which she pulled over her head.

Now all I need is some old boots and a woolly hat.

Lily shoved her feet into the smallest pair of boots she could find then tucked her hair under a knitted hat which she pulled well down over her forehead.

"Perfect!" she said, studying her reflection in the mirror.

*

"Tarrum-tum-tum!" Lily sang as she tramped through the forest.

She'd picked up a spare pickaxe at the door of the cottage and slung it over her shoulder. If she was going to do the disguise thing, she had to do it properly.

"Tarrum-tum . . ."

"Hush!" a man warned as Lily drew near to the palace. "No singing allowed!"

"Why not?" Lily asked in a gruff voice.

"The Princess is dead. The palace is in mourning."

So Queenie hadn't shared the happy news with poor King Jakob. As far as everyone else knew, Snow White was still dead.

Lily plodded on into the town that

squatted by the tall palace walls.

In the narrow streets women whispered on their doorsteps.

"The Queen is in a dreadful rage," they muttered. "She has flung Sir Manfred into the dungeons and will allow no one to speak of the poor dead Princess!"

Lily walked on. She only stopped when she came to the wide palace gates.

"Who goes there?" a sentry cried, stepping out with his spear to block Lily.

"My name is Joe," Lily croaked. "I have come from the land beyond Ice Mountain to visit my sister, Nurse Gretchen."

Quick thinking, Lil! So far, so good. No one had recognised her or even paused to give her a second glance.

"No visitors!" the sentry snapped.

"Haven't you heard, the palace is in mourning for the death of the Princess?"

"But I have journeyed a great distance," Lily protested. She kept her hat well down over her forehead and took her axe from her shoulder and rested on it as she'd seen the dwarves do. "My sister has waited a whole year to see me."

"No visitors," the sentry said again, his mouth snapping shut like a letter-box on a strong spring.

"Very well," Lily said gruffly. She knew of a back entrance to the palace. With luck she would be able to slip in unnoticed.

The sentry watched her walk away with narrowed, suspicious eyes.

8

Lily was in luck.

She trudged around the palace walls to the small back entrance where there was no sentry on duty.

Knock-knock! She banged on the wooden door, and when no one came, she tested the handle.

Cool! The door opened. Lily the dwarf stepped inside.

"There, there, my dove, my dear!" a familiar voice cooed, and Lily saw a stout woman in a plain green skirt with a brown shawl wrapped around her shoulders, comforting a girl crying by the open fire.

Gretchen! Straight away Lily recognised Snow White's old nurse.

Gretchen hadn't heard Lily come into the kitchen. "Dry your eyes, my little chicken. These tears will do no good."

"Oh but, my poor, poor Will!" the girl sobbed. She raised her apron and hid her face. "The Queen has thrown him in a dark dungeon with horrible thick walls, where the rats run over his feet and there is no window to let in the light. Whatever will become of him?"

This is Melina, Lily realised. *And whoa, what's this about Will being locked up?*

"Hush, my sparrow. We will go to the King and tell him what has befallen your young man. I'm sure His Most Royal Highness will soon set him free."

Melina dried her eyes and sniffed back her tears. She looked up at Gretchen. "It is worse than you think, Nurse! The Queen has accused my poor Will of being the monster who led Snow White into the forest to kill her!"

"Hush!" Gretchen said, less firmly than before.

"But Will is a good man. He would never do such a thing," Melina said, beginning to cry all over again.

"Indeed he would not!" Lily spoke out at last. She kept her head down and her voice gruff. "I speak for my brother, Will – he is brave and true!"

"Your brother!" Melina cried, springing up from her seat. "Then you have come to save him, like the others?"

Lily stepped back quickly. As Melina threw herself at her, Lily's hat slipped back. Lily grabbed it and pulled it down once more.

"Which brother are you?" Melina asked. "Are you Jack, whom Will always speaks of with such pride? Or Tom, who is steady as a rock and will never let you down?"

"My name is Joe," Lily said, thrusting her chin out and squaring her shoulders.

Melina looked puzzled. "Joe? Will has never spoken of you."

"Never mind that," Lily said quickly. She saw that Gretchen was looking at her with great interest. "You say the others are already here?"

"To be sure." Gretchen bustled forward. "Not half an hour since, they marched into the courtyard demanding to see the King."

Lily turned to the Nurse. "Will you take me to them, my good woman?" *That's what they said in the bad old days when they were talking to a servant – "My good woman", "My good man"!* Lily hoped she'd got it right, except for the slight squeak in her voice.

Gretchen nodded then turned back to Melina. "Wait here, my dove. I will take Joe through the great hall, out into the courtyard. The brothers will talk to His Most Royal Highness and persuade him to set Will free. Then I will return here with the good news."

Full of tears and sobs, Melina nodded. "Please let it happen!" she sighed.

"And so . . . Joe, you are the youngest of the brothers?" Gretchen asked as she led Lily along a dark corridor.

"How can you tell?" Lily grunted.

"Why, because you have no beard on your smooth chin, and because you have a piping voice," the Nurse replied.

"I am the youngest," Lily agreed. She pulled her shirt collar up around her cheeks and strode along with giant steps.

"And you truly believe you can set Will free?"

"I can!" Lily squeaked. She cleared her

throat. "My brother will be free before you know it!"

For Lily had a plan.

"The dungeons are cold and dark," Gretchen went on, her skirt rustling as she waddled along. "I know it for a fact – because the Queen once saw fit to put me there."

"I remember that . . ." Lily said before she could stop herself.

"You do?" Gretchen stopped and turned her wrinkled gaze on Lily.

"Yes. That is, I heard my brother Will tell the story of how you were thrown in the dungeon because you had displeased the Queen." Trying not to blush at her mistake, Lily strode ahead. "He heard the tale from Melina, of course."

"Well, well, news travels far and wide," Gretchen tutted.

Oops – nearly! Lily thought. She was building herself up to the moment when she could stand in the courtyard alongside Jack and the rest and King Jakob himself would appear.

That'll be the time to do it! The King will be sad and lonely and the dwarves will be trying to convince him that Will isn't a murderer.

"Far and wide indeed," Gretchen muttered as she opened the door on to the yard.

Then I'll take off my hat and my jacket and leggings, Lily decided. *And underneath will be my Snow White clothes, and I'll puff out my skirt and shake myself down . . . and finally I'll walk straight up to the King!*

9

"Pray, who are you?" Her Most Royal Highness's voice rang out in the courtyard.

"Your Majesty, my name is Jack. These are my brothers, Tom, Roly, Pete, Hans and Walt. We wish you to set free Will the miner, who at this moment lies in your dungeon." Jack's reply was bold and unafraid.

"And how may you hope to bring about this villain's release?" Queen Serena sneered.

"We are here to see His Most Royal Highness, King Jakob. His Majesty will listen to reason."

Inside the great hall, Lily stopped in her tracks. She closed her eyes and took a deep breath.

"The King cannot come," Queenie replied haughtily. "As you know, he is in mourning for his dear daughter, Princess Snow White, who died a most cruel death at your brother's hands. You must speak to me instead."

Uh-oh! Lily thought. *Trust Queenie to poke her nose in before the dwarves can get to the King! No way am I going to show myself while she's around! No way at all!*

So Lily hid behind the heavy oak door and listened instead.

"Come!" Nurse Gretchen hissed, still anxious to reunite Joe with his brothers.

"N-O, no!" Lily mouthed back, dragging Gretchen into hiding with her.

"Your Most Royal Highness," Jack went on. "My brother Will stands accused of the Princess's murder, but we are here to tell you that he is innocent."

Pete stepped forward. "Will did nothing wrong," he insisted. "Here are six witnesses to testify that he did not leave the cottage on the night that the Princess disappeared."

Lily bit her lip. It would be so easy for the dwarves to give her away, to tell the truth about how they had taken her in and hidden her and so prove that their brother was not guilty of murder!

"Silence!" Her Most Royal Highness ordered.

Through a crack in the door, Lily saw Queenie rush at Pete and seize him by the shoulder. "You are all in league with your treacherous brother. Guards, come quickly!"

At the Queen's angry call, ten men with

spears ran into the courtyard and pointed their weapons at the dwarves.

"Take them all to the dungeons!" Queen

Serena shrieked, turning quickly and striding away. Her black velvet cloak billowed out behind her like bats' wings. "Lock them up! Give them no food or water until they confess!"

The loyal dwarves still did not betray Snow White. Their goodness and bravery

brought tears to Lily's eyes.

Gretchen handed her a coarse handkerchief and stared harder than ever.

As the guards marched the six brothers

away to the dungeons, Queen Serena rushed through the door into the great hall. Her face was pale with fury. "Fetch Sir Manfred from the dungeon!" she shrieked. "Prince Lovelace! Where are those two fools when I call?"

Soon Lily heard footsteps running along the gallery and snatched a glimpse of Manfred and Prince Pester-Face, hurrying to answer the Queen.

"Your Majesty!"

"Your Most Royal Highness!" they said as they fell to their knees and cowered before her.

Queenie hauled Manfred back to his feet. "Quickly, go and tell the King that I have arrested six thieves. They have stolen gold from our gold mines and must pay for it with their lives!"

"B-b-but!" Nurse Gretchen was about to step out from behind the door, until Lily stopped her.

Next Her Most Royal Highness dragged Prince Lovelace upright. "And you, you lily-livered creature," she spat. "You must ride to their cottage and find a gold nugget there. Bring it back here as proof!"

"W-w-where shall I search, Your Majesty?" Pester-Face stammered.

"Anywhere – everywhere!" Queenie screeched. "These men are gold miners – they must keep gold nuggets in their cottage. I don't care how you do it, but bring me back the proof I need!"

Scared out of their wits, the two men fled. Meanwhile, the Queen stomped up the stairs and along the gallery.

"Oh my, oh my!" Nurse Gretchen gasped. "Seven dwarves in the dungeon, all about to lose their heads!"

"Hush!" Lily was stunned by what she had just seen. "We have to keep ours – I mean, stay calm and do something to set them free – and fast!"

But just then, Prince Lovelace came scuttling back into the hall. "Gold!" he declared, turning this way and that. "I must find gold!" Then he spied Lily the dwarf.

"Uh-oh!" Lily muttered, turning and running out of the door.

"Come back!" the Prince cried, mistaking Lily for one of the dwarves. "Guards, one has escaped! Stop, thief!"

92

With his long, spindly legs, Lovelace soon caught up with Lily. "You shall not get away!" he declared, seizing her by the arm.

As Lily twisted and pulled herself free, her hat fell back and Prince Lovelace gawped.

"Y-y-you are . . ." he gasped.

"No, I'm not!" she argued, tugging until the Prince let go of her shirtsleeve. "I'm Joe, the dwarf – OK!"

"Snow White – my dove, my dear!" Nurse Gretchen whispered in amazement.

Scrabbling to grab her again, Lovelace caught hold of Lily's gold necklace and wrenched it from her neck. But she had no time to snatch it back. Instead, she made a run for it, across the cobbled

yard, out through the main gates before
the sentries appeared.

*

Back in the cottage, Lily sat down and
drew breath.

That turned out great! she told herself.
*Now everyone's in prison and Pester-Face has
got my gold locket!*

Looking round the empty kitchen, she
saw seven pickaxes leaning against the
wall and seven lamps arranged in a

row on the windowsill.

"The house feels so empty!" she sighed, getting up and wandering into the big bedroom, where seven nightcaps hung on seven hooks and seven beds were neatly made.

"OK, there's only one thing to do!" Lily spoke out loud to convince herself. "I have to get changed back into my Snow White outfit then go to the palace to give myself up!"

*

As Lily got changed, she thought of all the reasons why she had to return:

1 – The dwarves did nothing wrong. In fact, they did everything right.

2 – Queenie is crazy, and cruel enough to have them all killed.

3 – Pester-Face will recognise the "SW" on my locket.

4 – He'll show it to the Queen.

5 – Queenie already knows I'm alive, so, in the long run, the game's up anyway.

Slowly and fearfully, Lily took off her leggings and shirt. She puffed out the skirt she'd been wearing underneath. But when she looked in the mirror it was so creased she was ashamed to be seen, so she put on her flowered apron to cover the creases.

"Better!" she said, trying not to let her top lip quiver.

She must set off for the palace straight away and sneak in the back way. She would seek out Gretchen, who had surely already seen through her disguise.

Together they would work out a way of getting to see the King.

Be brave! Lily told herself, taking one last look in the mirror.

But in the reflection she could see her bedroom window, and beyond that a woman collecting firewood in the clearing.

The woman was bent and old. Lily could hear her muttering to herself as she picked up sticks. So she turned from the mirror and hurried to the door.

97

"It's enough to send a poor soul to her grave," the old woman moaned. "The nights are long and cold. There is never enough wood for the fire."

"Here," Lily told her, walking briskly towards the woodshed. "We have plenty. Help yourself."

"You are very kind," the old woman croaked, still stooping and keeping her shawl over her head so that her face was covered. She peered into the shed at the pile of logs. "Tell me, my dear, what is your name?"

10

"My name is Snow White," Lily told her. She wouldn't have come out with it, except she had a lot on her mind.

"A pretty name for a very pretty girl," the old wood gatherer went on. "My dear, may I put down my bundle and rest a while?"

"As long as you like," Lily said. "But I have to dash."

"Oh my old bones!" the woman sighed. She sat down on the ground beside the shed, her back bent and her face still hidden. "They ache so. Ah, you will see, my dear, that life is cruel when you are no longer young and beautiful!"

Quickly Lily added some logs to the old woman's bundle. "There!" she said. "I must go now, like I said."

"Then help me to my feet," came the croaky request. "For I am old and my bones creak."

What next? Lily thought as she pulled the wizened creature up. *I have to leave now!*

"Ouch!" the old woman cried as she stood up. "Oh my dear, I am caught on a sharp thorn!"

"OK, hold still – I'll unhook you," Lily offered. This was getting a bit too much – you did one thing for the poor old thing and she wanted half a dozen others!

Still, Lily inspected the old grey shawl wrapped around the woman's shoulders and saw that there was a black twig with nasty thorns sticking to it.

"Take care!" the old woman warned. "The thorns are sharp!"

Lily leaned forward. Carefully she took hold of the twig.

Then something weird happened. The old woman stood up straight and tall. She grasped Lily's hand with strong fingers, guided it towards a sharp thorn and made her grasp it.

"Ouch!" Lily cried as the thorn pricked

her forefinger and drew a drop of bright red blood.

She looked up at the face of the old wood gatherer and saw that it bore the features of Queen Serena.

"Snow White, you are a foolish girl!" Queenie cried, throwing off her shawl to reveal a black gown and ruby necklace. "So innocent and easy to trick!"

"Oh!" Lily groaned. She stared at her finger and felt her knees grow weak.

"The thorn bears deadly poison!" Her Most Royal Highness cried in triumph.

Lily's head went woozy and everything swam before her eyes. She saw the blood red rubies sparkle at the cruel Queen's throat.

Lily sank to her knees. Her Most Royal Highness gazed down with ice in her heart.

"Let Will go," Lily pleaded as she swooned. "And the rest – Jack and Tom, Roly . . . Pete, Hans . . . and Walt!"

Lily drifted off into a world filled with white.

The whiteness dazzled her then turned silvery. It was like being inside a cloud way out in space – weightless, floating.

"Lily!" Amber and Pearl cried.

They'd been waiting for this moment when the white light blinded them and silver dust fell on to the basement floor.

Lily heard her friends' voices before she saw them. Sounds came to her faintly, from a long way off. She was still floating, being lowered gently to the ground.

"You were away for ages!" Pearl complained.

Lily opened her eyes at last and looked up.

"What kept you?" Amber demanded, snapping her fingers in front of Lily's face to make sure she was properly awake.

"I finally met the dwarves," Lily explained. "They were so-o-o cool!"

"Come on, get up!" Pearl urged. "What's this flowery thing you're wearing?"

Groggily Lily got to her feet. "It's an apron," she replied. "I made it out of an old curtain."

"What else?" Amber demanded. She didn't want to hear boring stuff about aprons. She wanted the low-down on the Wicked Queen.

"I brushed their floor and darned their socks," Lily said dreamily.

"Fascinating!" Amber groaned.

"Hans made me a gold locket with my initials on."

"Where, where?" Pearl demanded.

Gently touching the place on her neck

where the locket had rested, Lily sighed. "I lost it in a fight with Prince Pester-Face. And this is exactly how it happened . . ."

Have you checked out...

www.dressingupdreams.net

It's the place to go for games, downloads, activities, sneak previews and lots of fun!

You'll find a special dressing-up game and lots of activities and fun things to do, as well as news on Dressing-Up Dreams and all your favourite characters.

Sign up to the newsletter at **www.dressingupdreams.net** to receive extra clothes for your Dressing-Up Dreams doll and the opportunity to enter special members only competitions.

What happens next...?
Log on to www.dressingupdreams.net for a sneak preview of my next adventure!

CAN YOU SPOT THE TWO DIFFERENCES AND THE HIDDEN LETTER IN THESE TWO PICTURES OF LILY?

There is a spot-the-difference picture and hidden letter in the back of all four Dressing-Up Dreams books about Lily (look for the books with 5, 6, 7 or 8 on the spine). Hidden in one of the pictures above is a secret letter. Find all four letters and put them together to make a special Dressing-Up Dreams word, then send it to us. Each month, we will put the correct entries in a draw and one lucky winner will receive a magical Dressing-Up Dreams goodie bag including an exclusive Dressing-Up Dreams keyring!

Send your magical word, your name, age and address
on a postcard to: **Lily's Dressing-Up Dreams Competition**

UK Readers:	**Australian Readers:**	**New Zealand Readers:**
Hodder Children's Books	Hachette Children's Books	Hachette Livre NZ Ltd
338 Euston Road	Level 17/207 Kent Street	PO Box 100 749
London NW1 3BH	Sydney NSW 2000	North Shore City 0745
kidsmarketing@hodder.co.uk	childrens.books@hachette.com.au	childrensbooks@hachette.co.nz

Only one entry per child. Final draw: 30th August 2009
For full terms and conditions go to www.hachettechildrens.co.uk/terms

COLOURING FUN!

Carefully colour the Dressing-Up Dreams picture on the next page and then send it in to us.

Or you can draw your very own fairytale character. You might want to think about what they would wear or if they have special powers.

Each month, we will put the best entries on the website gallery and one lucky winner will receive a magical Dressing-Up Dreams goodie bag!

Send your drawing, your name, age and address on a postcard to:
Lily's Dressing-Up Dreams Competition

UK Readers:
Hodder Children's Books
338 Euston Road
London NW1 3BH
kidsmarketing@hodder.co.uk

Australian Readers:
Hachette Children's Books
Level 17/207 Kent Street
Sydney NSW 2000
childrens.books@hachette.com.au

New Zealand Readers:
Hachette Livre NZ Ltd
PO Box 100 749
North Shore City 0745
childrensbooks@hachette.co.nz